THIS CANDLEWICK BOOK BELONGS TO:

_____

_____

_____

To my sweet baby ONI (my moomie) —W. M.

To my mom — Grandma Gerry, as she's called
by all the kids she's read to over the years — P. R.

Text copyright © 2012 by Wynton Marsalis
Illustrations copyright © 2012 by Paul Rogers

First paperback edition 2021

Library of Congress Cataloging-in-Publication Data is available.

Library of Congress Catalog Card Number 2011048367

ISBN 978-0-7636-3991-4 (hardcover)
ISBN 978-1-5362-2196-1 (paperback)

APS 26 25 24 23 22 21
10 9 8 7 6 5 4 3 2 1

Printed in Humen, Dongguan, China

This book was hand-lettered and typeset in Glypha and Caslon 540.
The illustrations were done in ink and finished digitally.
Book design by Jill von Hartmann

Candlewick Press
99 Dover Street
Somerville, Massachusetts 02144

visit us at www.candlewick.com

Squeak, RUMBLE, WHOMP! WHOMP! WHOMP!

a sonic adventure by

Wynton Marsalis

illustrated by

Paul Rogers

CANDLEWICK PRESS

Our back door squeeeaks.

A nosy
mouse
eeek-eeek-eeeks!

It's also how my sister's saxophone sometimes *speee....eaks.*

Big trucks on the highway *RRRR*

Hunger makes my tummy GR*rru*MB*le*.

UMBLE.

tluck…tlock

tluck…tlock… Our faucet
needs
a fix.

TLICK - TLOCK

TLICK - TLOCK

My alarm
clock ticks.

tlock

tlaack

tlack

tlick!

Pizzicato violinists plick-pluck licks.

WOoo-uuu, oooo-uuu

Ambulances say.

MMMrrrrrrrr

A motorcycle speeds away.

Brrraaomp!

The trombone
slides down
to play.

I love the wind *whistling* across my face,

whooooo-ushing my kite into outer space.

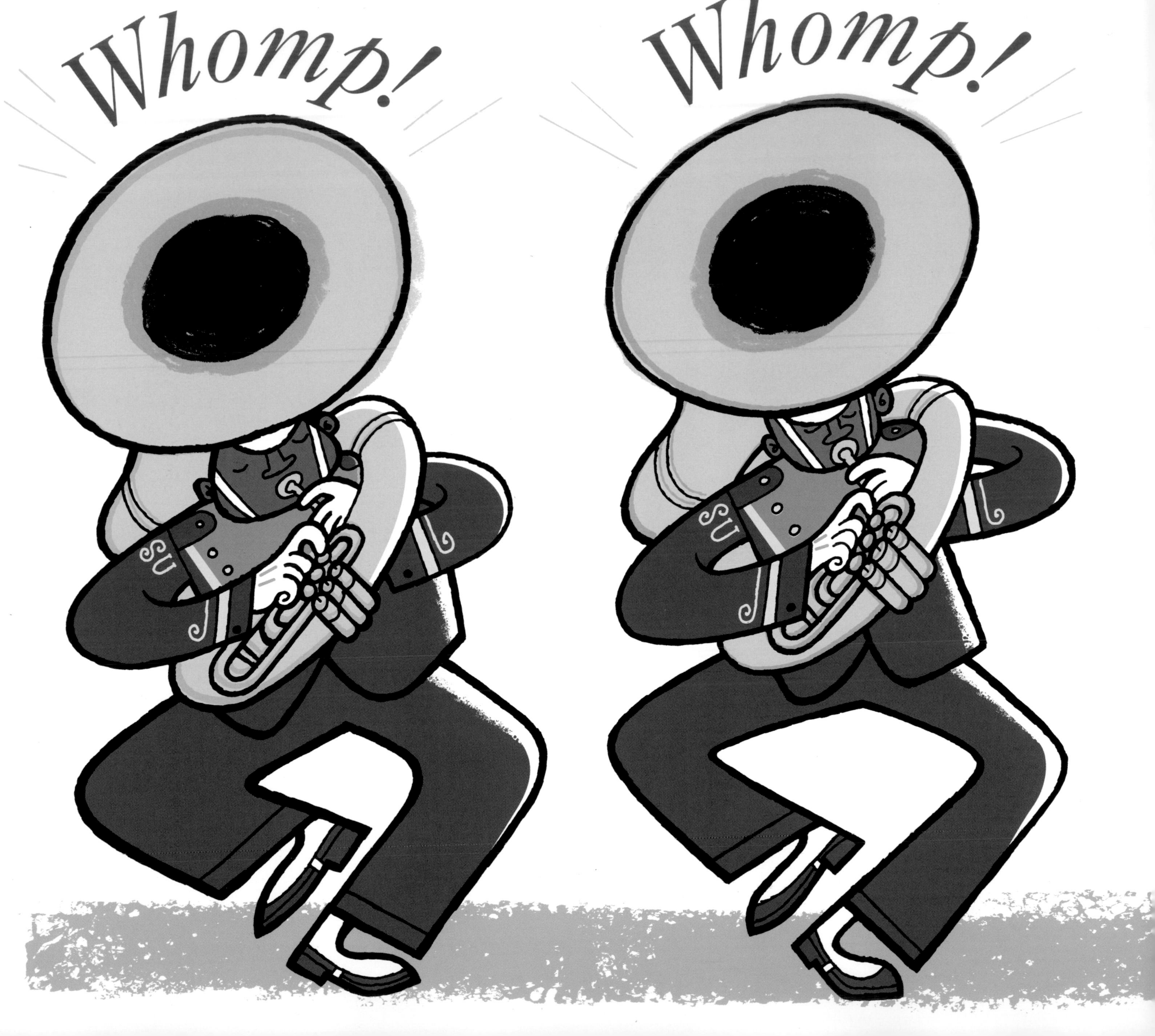
Whomp!
Whomp!
SU
SU

Chrrrick chrrrick chrrrick chrrrick
—buttering my toast.

Krrrick krrrick krrrick krrrick
—quick where it itches the most.

*Schuk-chuk,
schuk-chuk,
schuka
chuk,
sschick.*

Hear that
washboard boast.

Ting, tink-y, ting, tap!

Flies *bzzz bzzz bzzz* all around my food.

The barber's clippers *Jurrr! Jurrr! Jurrr!* And I'm cool, dude.

The
Big
Train
rolls
down
the

WAAAA!
BAAAW!
track.

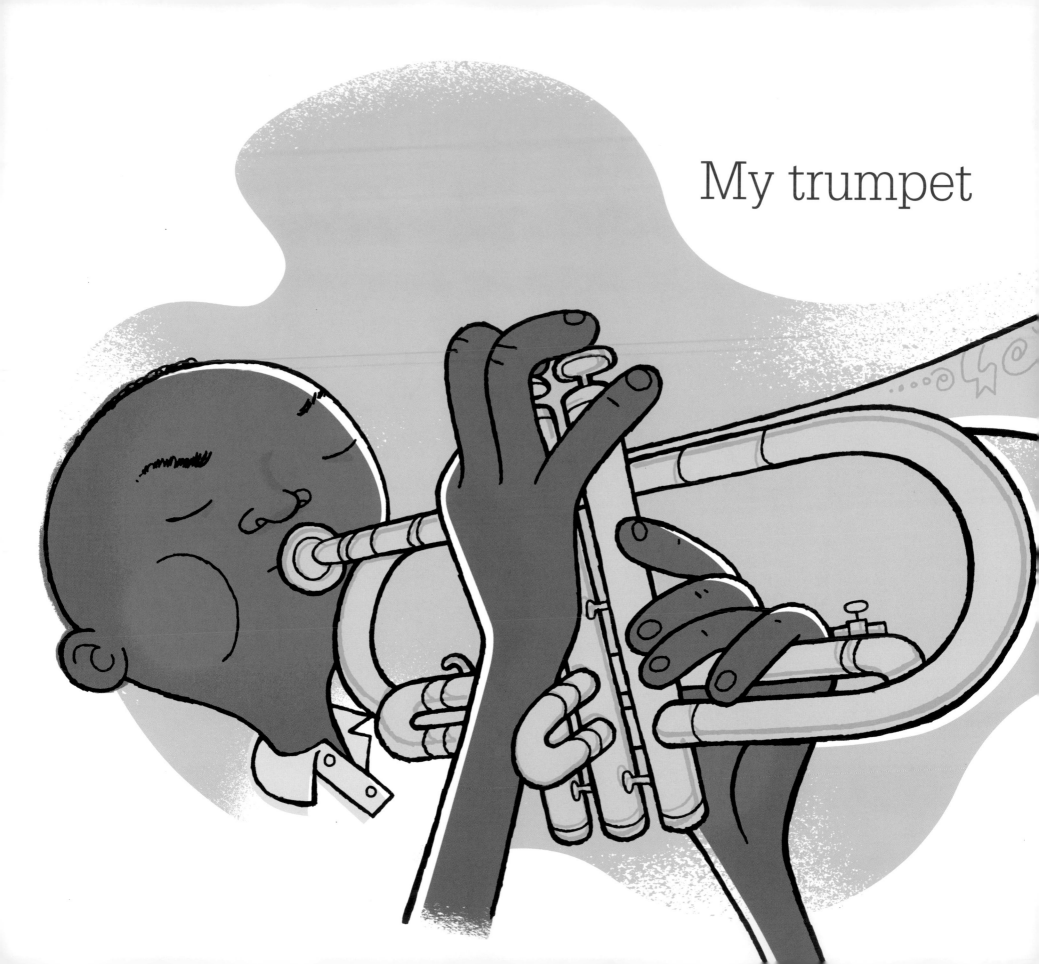

My trumpet

Blaa
BLAA
BLAAARES

with a
BIG OL'
attack!

Wynton Marsalis is an internationally acclaimed musician, composer, and tireless champion of jazz. He is the recipient of a Pulitzer Prize and the winner of nine Grammy Awards, and he was honored with the National Humanities Medal in 2015. The artistic director for the Jazz at Lincoln Center program, he lives in New York City.

Paul Rogers has created everything from billboard portraits at Dodger Stadium to a silkscreen portrait of Wynton Marsalis for the New Orleans Jazz & Heritage Festival. He lives in Pasadena, California, where he is on the faculty of ArtCenter College of Design.